MW00898324

Duck Sees the Rain

Written by Margo Gates

Illustrated by Carol Herring

GRL Consultants, Diane Craig and Monica Marx,
Certified Literacy Specialists

Lerner Publications ◆ Minneapolis

Lerner Publications Company
A division of Lerner Publishing Group, Inc.
241 First Avenue North
Minneapolis, MN 55401 USA

For reading levels and more information, look up this title at www.lernerbooks.com.

Main body text set in Mikado 24/41
Typeface provided by Hannes von Doehren.

The images in this book are used with the permission of: Carol Herring.

Library of Congress Cataloging-in-Publication Data

Names: Gates, Margo, author. | Herring, Carol, illustrator.
Title: Duck sees the rain / by Margo Gates ; illustrated by Carol Herring.
Description: Minneapolis : Lerner Publications, [2020] | Series: Let's look at weather
    (Pull ahead readers - Fiction) | Includes index.
Identifiers: LCCN 2018057290 (print) | LCCN 2018057760 (ebook) | ISBN 9781541562134
    (eb pdf) | ISBN 9781541558397 (lb : alk. paper) | ISBN 9781541573161 (pb : alk. paper)
Subjects: LCSH: Readers (Primary) | Ducks—Juvenile fiction. | Rain and rainfall—Juvenile
    fiction.
Classification: LCC PE1119 (ebook) | LCC PE1119 .G3839 2020 (print) | DDC 428.6—dc23

LC record available at https://lccn.loc.gov/2018057290

Manufactured in the United States of America
1 – CG – 7/15/19

Contents

Duck Sees the Rain

Duck sees the sky.

Duck sees the clouds.

Duck sees the rain.

Duck sees the puddle.

Duck sees the sun.

Duck sees the rainbow.

Did You See It?

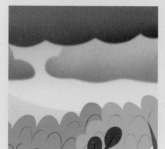
clouds

puddle

rain

rainbow

sky

sun

Index

16